W9-BIZ-003

Brigitte Weninger was born in Kufstein, Austria, and spent twenty years working as a kindergarten teacher before trying her hand at writing. She has since published more than fifty books, which have been translated into thirty languages worldwide. She continues to be heavily involved in promoting literacy and storytelling.

Eve Tharlet was born in France but spent much of her childhood in Germany. After graduating from the Superior School of Decorative Arts in Strasbourg, France, she began working as a freelance illustrator in 1981 and quickly received international acclaim. Her big breakthrough came with the series about Davy, the cute and cheeky bunny, which propelled her name around the world.

First published in Switzerland under the title *Schöne Ferien, Pauli!*

Translated by David Henry Wilson.

First published in the United States, Great Britain, Canada, Australia, and New Zealand in 2018 by NorthSouth Books, Inc., an imprint of NordSüd Verlag AG, CH-8050 Zürich, Switzerland.

Distributed in the United States by NorthSouth Books, Inc., New York 10016.
Library of Congress Cataloging-in-Publication Data is available.
ISBN: 978-0-7358-4278-6 (trade edition)
1 3 5 7 9 • 10 8 6 4 2
Printed in Germany by Grafisches Centrum Cuno GmbH & Co. KG, 2017.
www.northsouth.com

Brigitte Weninger
Eve Tharlet

Davy's Summer Vacation!

North
South

Davy was playing beside the pond with his toy rabbit, Nicky, when Wendy Wildgoose landed next to them.

"How are you doing?" asked Davy.

"I went on a fantastic trip with my family," said Wendy. "We visited the Big Water. We swam, played in the sand, and saw all kinds of new things."

Davy let out a sigh. "I wish I could go on a trip like that!"

"But you can't fly," gabbled the goose.

"It's true," grumbled Davy. "Rabbits don't have wings ... but we have strong legs."

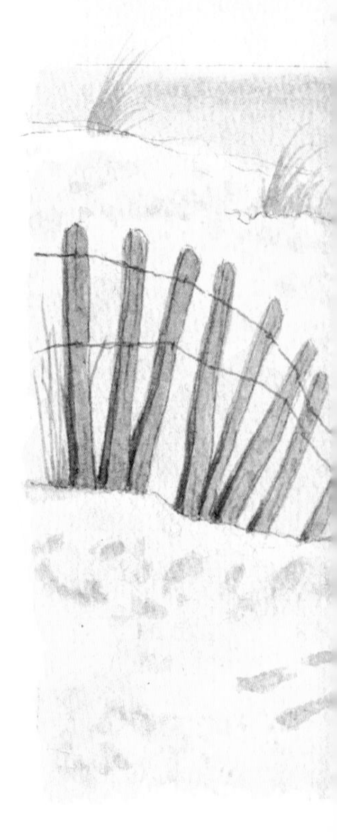

Davy's family was playing the memory game with leaves when Davy rushed into the room, shouting, "Ple-e-ease, Dad, ple-e-ease, Mom, I want to travel too and see lots of new things!"

"What on Earth made you think of that?" asked Mother Rabbit.

"Wendy Wildgoose has just been telling me about the Big Water," said Davy. "You can swim and play in the sand and eat lots of fine food. Please can we go there?"

"Hmmm, sounds nice," murmured Father Rabbit. "I've sometimes thought about it myself. Well, yes, why not?"

“Yippee, yahoo, yeehaw! We’re going to the Big Water!” cried Davy, Manni, Lina, Max, and Mia. And they hopped around the room in sheer delight.

Only Mother Rabbit shook her head doubtfully. “But it’s a VERY long way. . . .”

"That doesn't matter," cried Davy, hugging his mother. "The farther away the better. Let's go pack our things!"

7

The young rabbits packed buckets and shovels, toy boats, fairy-tale books, dolls, footballs, goggles, fishing nets, and of course plenty of treats!

Mother and Father Rabbit had other important things to think about: food, blankets and pillows, clothes for warm weather, clothes for cold weather, this, that, and more besides.

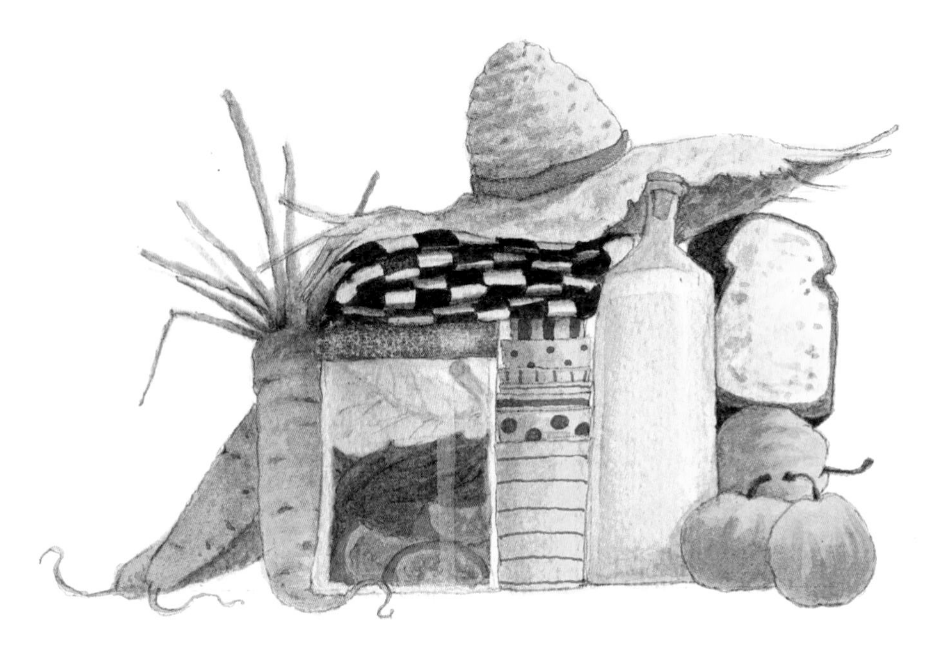

At last they'd packed it all, and Mother Rabbit called out, "Children, are you ready? Bring your bags to the front door."

"By all the fir cones in the forest," cried Father Rabbit, "I never knew we had so many possessions!"

"How are we going to carry them all?" asked Max.

"I know!" said Davy. "We'll pack them on our wagon."

7

They finished loading the wagon. Davy had one last thing to add: his little toy rabbit.

But just as he did—CRAAACKKK! All four wheels broke off!

"Pigs, pigeons, and porcupines!" yelled Davy, and he gave the wagon a kick.

"Now what are we going to do?" whined Lina, Manni, and Mia.

Just then the mail delivery bunny came around the corner.

"Maybe we can mail our luggage to the Big Water," suggested Max.

The delivery bunny ran his tape measure around the pile of bags and scribbled a few numbers on a piece of paper. "That will cost you three carrot bucks for each small bag and five for each large one. Altogether ... one hundred carrot bucks."

"That's a fortune!" cried Mother and Father Rabbit. "We can't afford to pay that. Come on, children—we'll take all our things back indoors."

"Oh no!" cried the children. "It's sooo BORING here! We want to go somewhere different and see new things!"

"But we can't," said Father Rabbit. "I'm so sorry."

Sadly the children carried their bags back into the burrow.

While Davy was dragging his umbrella back into the burrow, he accidentally knocked a leaf off the tree. It looked like a little heart, and floated down to land at Davy's feet.

It gave him a wonderful idea.

"Mother! Father! Come here, everybody! I know what we can do...."

"What? Where? How?"

"It'll be a surprise!" Davy laughed. "I'll show you. All we need is our strong rabbit legs, a blanket, lots of nice things to eat, and our buckets and shovels."

"Well, that's easy enough," said Mother with a smile.

"But where are we going?" asked his brothers and sisters.

Davy didn't tell them. As soon as they'd collected all the things he'd mentioned, he simply marched off.

He led the family across flowering meadows, through a forest, and over a little hill. It was quite a long journey, but it was also very beautiful.

Everywhere they went there were so many new things to see!

But eventually, little Mia began to complain. “I’m tired. Are we there yet?”

“Yes,” said Davy, and brushed a couple of branches to one side. “NOW we’re there.”

"WOW! This is great!" they shouted.

The family sat down on the warm sand, dipped their legs in the blue spring water, and snacked from Mother's picnic basket.

"This is a real vacation paradise!" said Father Rabbit. "There can't be anywhere more beautiful than this!"

"But where are we?" Mother wanted to know.

“We’re right in the middle of the world,” said Davy proudly. “Grandpa showed me this place once. He used to play here when he was just a little rabbit. It’s a bit too far to come here often, but today we made it!”

“So we’ve been on a long trip after all!” Mother laughed.

"Grandpa also told me a secret," said Davy. "This is a magic spring. If you put a heart-shaped leaf in the water and make a nice wish, your wish will come true. Do you want to try?"

Each of them looked for a heart-shaped leaf and slid it into the water.

Mia's leaf was the first to float away, and she said, "I wish we could come back soon to the middle of the world."

"Hey, that's what I was going to wish. . . ."

"Me too . . ."

Davy laughed. "So this summer we're going to see lots and lots of new things. Happy summer vacation!"